For my parents, who taught me to see beyond appearances
and for Billie, whose color never mattered at all - A.C.

For my beautiful wife Nina, who always believes in me - D.S.

Precious Little Books
www.preciouslittlebooks.com

Designed by Nina Tara

Printing and binding: TSE Worldwide Press, Inc.

Printed in China

ISBN 0-9787235-0-3

People Are So Different!

Ann Clarke
Illustrated by Duncan Smith

PRECIOUS
LITTLE
BOOKS

Everywhere we go,
people are so different . . .

Some are very **BIG**

and some are small.

Some people are black,
some are brown,
and others are not dark at all.

Some people are
and some are red,
but no one is green?

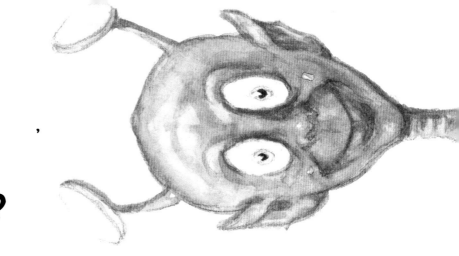

Some people are **TALL**,

while other's are short.

Some people are pretty
and other's are not.

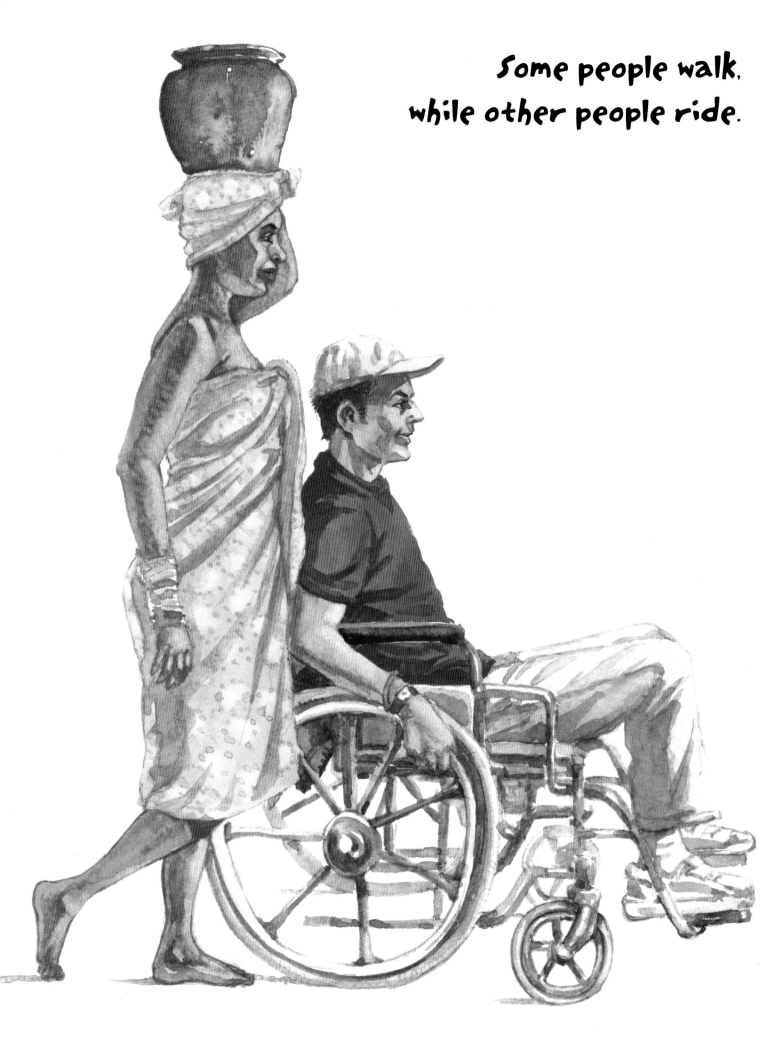

Some people walk,
while other people ride.

Some people are old,
while other people are young!

All the different people,
smile when they get a hug.

All the different people
cry if they get hurt.

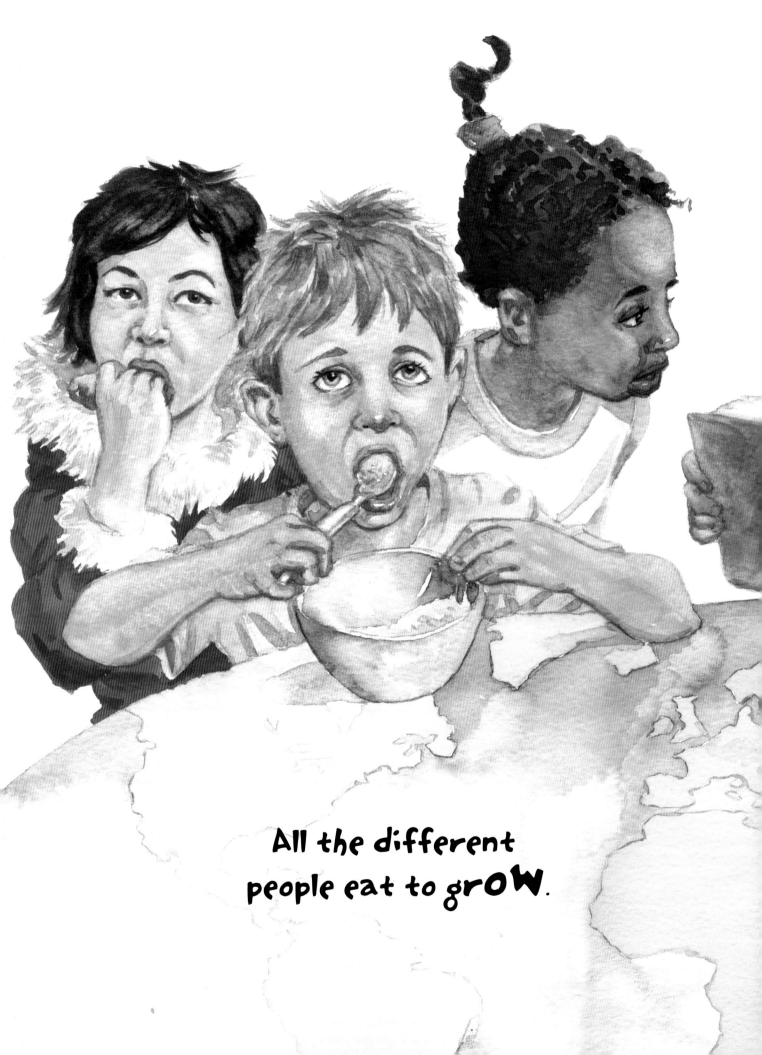

All the different
people eat to grOW.

And all the different people
read books to know.

All the different people,
like to have friends.

And all the different people are sad
if nobody plays with them.

So on the outside while we are
all so different as can be,

Inside, all the different people,
are really JUST LIKE ME!

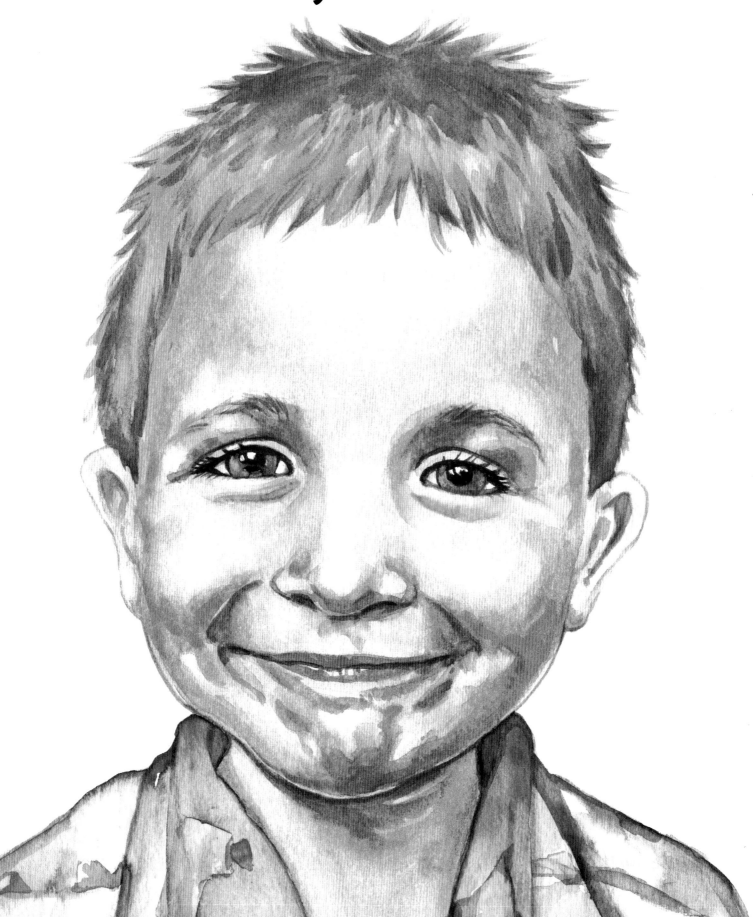